"A Good fight does not require dying, while trying to live"

HANDS OF ABUSE, THE UNFORESEEN TRUTH

How Domestic Violence Changed my Life

Angela D. Thompson

My Dream, My Vision

This book is dedicated to all the women of the world who have experienced abuse, and any form of abuse.

Stand up for your children, stand up for yourself. Walk away, before you're carried away. Find GOD and you find your journey, and within that journey you find LIFE.

With Love My Sisters,
Angela

Table of Contents

Acknowledgments

God

To my Lord and Savior, through your footprint I have been able to call myself a survivor, you have given me strength to reach for the unknown, and you have empowered me to look further than I can see. I will continue to build through you, because my path is not finished. Never have you forsaken me, and I know you never will. Thank You.

My Husband

Without you, I could not have seen a clearer path. Those were your hands that pushed me, while I staggered into the unknown. Through you came inspiration to not give up, to open my eyes to see the BIGGER picture. YOU were the inspiration for me to complete my journey in writing my book, and you have shown me to not give up, despite our transgressions, and I Thank you.

Mom

There is no me without you mother, you have been the shield in my life that has protected me, from the tremendous stones thrown at me through life. When I fall you are there to pick me up, and because of you, I am still standing.

Through a strong generation of women, I have become ALL of you. Through your strength, I am still building my legacy. You know when I need you, and that is without me saying a word, and I Thank you.

Daddy

To my loving father, you are an inspiration and have been all my life. You have never given up on anything you have done. You have instilled in me, to never quit, and to keep pushing no matter how hard it gets. You told me to keep amazing you, and with that, I can only continue my journey, in that way, and I Thank you.

My Children

You two (Mon-Che' and Jalyn), are the reasons that I breathe, the reasons that I fight for life, to show you that it is more out there than what I can ever give you. Beyond dreams are better dreams, and beyond that are bigger dreams. Keep reaching and never give up, respect and be respected. You guys are my thriving force; follow me in my path to the TOP. You can do anything through Christ, who strengthens you. I Love you.

Friends

I would like to express my gratitude to the many people who pushed me to never give up on my dream, and to finish my path, in completing this book; to all those who provided support, talked things over, read, wrote, offered comments, allowed me to quote their remarks and assisted in the editing, proofreading and design. Thank you!

Preface

She has not only been mentally abused, but physically to a point where she doesn't see the door in front of her, she doesn't see that there is a way out. Her dreams only consist of death and destruction. Not only to herself but her family, she has been beaten, even though physically, she has scars, black eyes, red rings around her neck, bruises, and busted lips. However, these are not visibly seen on the outside, these are scars that are engraved in her heart, her soul, and her mind. She feels worthless; she means nothing, not even to her children. She is asking God why am I here? What have I done to deserve all of this, especially when I give so much of myself to please him?

She is the abused that has already taken her life, because she can't take it anymore. Suicide was the picture within the frame on the wall. The pills she had taken were the light at the end of the tunnel. She is the one where her life has been taken by her abuser. She is dead; she can't speak her mind, or tell her children she loves them. The burden of her heart is within her child's mind, they are crying because mommy is not there to love them, or to give them what they need as they grow into young men and women.

She is the woman that overcame abuse, she is stellar, and she has learned that no one that loves her will hurt her. She has realized that love doesn't hurt; love heals the mind and the soul. She is the one that has peeled herself off the ground, wiped away her tears, and looked in the mirror only to see that she is worth more than pain. She realizes that she is a survivor, that at the end of the day she can smile, through the pain. She walks now in peace and not of turmoil. She holds her head up high, and her confidence is unbroken.

She is the one that has murder on her mind; she wants to kill what has hardened her heart. She only knows that the pain has to stop, and the way to end it is to end the soul of the devil. Who is the devil, you ask? He is the killer of souls, the merciless, and the one that has to die, because she is already dead. She wants to stop the madness, to stop the dreams, to stop this way of living. To fold the deck that she has been given in this life. This life she knows is a game, and she knows she has to be the one that win.

This story is my story; these are my feelings, and my pain. I dedicate this to my sisters' who need direction, who needs to know that there is a way out. That you can save yourself, and you can be saved. I have been where you are, and I refuse to go back. My heart is hardened just like yours; I too didn't see a way out. This life had driven me to nowhere, and if I hadn't found my way back. I too would be one of the lost, one of the dead, and one of the ones that would not have seen my children grow. I too have been raped by the man that I loved, not only physically but mentally. He raped my soul, my thirst for life, and my will to live. Look into my face and you can see yourself. Have a look on the other side of my mirror and you will see what I have become.

1
Initiation to Life

This is my life, my fears, and my story, about domestic violence. These are the challenges I faced in life, the many hard reflections of truth, growth, definition, and even heartache. As like many women in this world today; I stand looking in the mirror; and I'm not just looking at the outer shell of which I am; I am looking at what I am on the inside, and who I have become. Looking in the mirror is about seeing who you really are; and if you look deep within the layers of your inner soul. You will see just how lost you really are, you will see a much larger picture, and you will see that domestic violence is not a form of love, nor will it ever be. As I stand and look in my bathroom mirror, it looks to me, as if it was a two way mirror. As I placed my hand on the mirror, I touched the glass, and my body on the other side of the mirror would not move. It's as if my body is frozen in time, motionless, scared, ashamed, and hurt. All while my body on the other side of the mirror is moving. I am trapped in the mirror and see no way out, tears running down my face. I am beaten.

My heart is beating so fast that I had to grab hold to my sink. My eyes are red, my body trembling, and blood is running from my face. I could hear each tear as it hits the water below, everything was in slow motion. I looked into the mirror and ask. "Who are you?" as I sat there awaiting a reply. I have come to realization that this mirror is my strength; and that the person on the other side of the mirror is not who I really am. My soul is now in two parts. Who I am on this day, is who I had become, and I don't like what I see. I am transparent and lonely, looking for help, and an end to the beginning.

I was young, adventurous, and loving life as I knew loving life should be at such a sweet and tender age. I was only 14 years old at the time, full of excitement, and having the want, the need, and the will to know everything I possibly could about life. I was vibrant and smart, and I invited challenges on things I thought were impossible, and I wanted to achieve things that others couldn't. I was in middle school, overall a very good kid, it was the beginning of the school year and I was excited about embarking on my new journey in life, having new friends, playing sports, and of course boys. Even, though I had to walk blocks to school everyday. I was dressed to impress, had my own style. I had created a style that caused my fellow students to hate me, this only happened because they didn't know who I was, nor did they ever want to get to know me. That is when I knew there would be trouble; it was a group of girls that I couldn't figure out. They hated me and wanted to fight me every day, and I just wasn't sure why.

They would bully me everyday, it just wouldn't stop, and they would find a reason to fight me, because I was not like them. I felt they just wanted to break me; break me from the person of whom I had become, break me of the things my mother instilled in me, and who she raised me to be. In life you will be put through a test, and it will be up to you, on how you handle it. At that time all I could say is why? Why me? This was the beginning of change for me, the building blocks of life as I see it today. Who I had grown up to be was about to be challenged, and never a day in my 14 years of life, have I had to fight my own battles. Initially, this was a struggle for me, and I had to grow up very fast; I was literally fighting every day for years, trying to defend who I was as a person. Well, let's just say I had to fight every day to define who I was. This would lead to me fighting all my life.

It all started my seventh grade year and it was such an exciting time for me, I was looking forward to what was to come in life. It was unclear to me why I had to endure such misery when I was so happy, and I didn't bother anyone. Only until later, did I learn that the only reason I was being bullied is because, I had long hair, was light skinned, and was liked by the boys in school. I say this to say, bullying happens for many reasons, and all forms of bullying are wrong, and should be dealt with accordingly. Bullying is a form of abuse, it's not okay, and it can affect you for the rest of your life. Domestic violence is a form of bullying, and it doesn't stop until you stop it.

I was pushed down all the time; hair pulled, ridiculed, and lied on, every day. I'm not sure how I was able to endure all of that. Until, one day I was challenged to meet my bully at the diamond mound in the back of the school, after school. The class bell rang, as I got up out of my seat, she the (bully) met me at the door of my classroom, it seemed to be hundreds of kids down the hallway as if they new something was about to go down. All I could see is her finger in my face and she threatening me, telling me "I'm going to beat your ass after school," she said "Not to run home, because "I know where you live". That day seemed to fly by, I was nervous and scared, and I knew I had to fight her no matter what. I never fought a day in my life; and I didn't know what to do. My walk home was her walk home; she lived right around the corner from me. I knew that she wouldn't hold anything back; she fought all the time, and was just ruthless. This is a feeling that would become natural for me later in life, living everyday scared of what the next day would bring.

The end of the day bell rang, and my heart sank and started to beat uncontrollably fast. Since, I was really active in sports, I went down to the gym and changed out of my clothes, then headed straight out to the back of the school. Once there, it seemed to be hundreds of kids out there just waiting to watch me get beat up. I can remember a friend of mine running across the field calling my name, yelling to me that "She has a chain, she has a chain, wrapped around her hand", so he quickly ran across the street where he lived, and grabbed a leather bracelet that he had with spikes on it. All the while I'm standing there hoping she wouldn't show up. I could see him running back to me, and I can see her coming through the crowd. Shaking, I snapped the bracelet around my knuckles as quickly as I could. I just knew this was the only thing that could save me from the embarrassment of being beat up.

I was so scared and all I could see is people parting like the (Red Sea), at this point I am trembling with fear. Here she comes with the bike chain wrapped around her fist, just as he said. It was hanging to the ground, and bulging from her fist. I could see the look in her eyes that she was going to do some damage. She walked up to me mouth wide open; I was not sure what she was saying to me. I was in such a daze, I couldn't hear anything anymore, and everything went silent. I couldn't hear the crowd, or my friends. I hit her, knocked her down to the ground and just kept hitting her over and over and over again. I was too scared to stop, I knew if she got up that would be the end for me. The principal and a teacher pulled me off of her, and at that point; my life changed. I was no longer the same person that I was when I walked out onto that field. That fight gave me courage and showed me that if I was pushed to the limit I could WIN. I would take that learning experience and use it, however, there was a right way and a wrong way, and I used both.

Challenges like this in life are true life lessons, and it is up to you to decipher what to do with it. For me, it changed my life, it changed me from that nice little girl, who didn't bother anyone; to someone I really didn't want to be. I learned to stand up for myself and not take anything from anyone. These moments in life are lessons, to see if you are strong enough to learn from them. My brother may he (rest in peace) taught me to never give up in any situation. This proves to be key; even in my life today. Like most young ladies all I wanted was a good life, to be successful in life, and to marry the man of my dreams. I didn't have to be rich, but I wanted sanity and to be independent. I was a very wise young lady that was full of dreams, and had a true passion for life.

My passion was to be a successful defense attorney. A strong independent black attorney, winning the biggest defense cases this challenging world could bring my way. I wanted to know so much at this age that it took me faster then I really wanted to go. I was so in-quisitive, wanting to know how everything worked. There was noth-ing I couldn't do, if I pushed hard enough, and studied even harder. However, my free spirit ways was sending me down a path, I knew nothing about and was unknown to me; it would turn out to be a self-destruction, a world wind of hurt, and make me question my will to live. Even though I had many friends that I could go places with, and do the things I wanted to do, I wanted to be like them. I wanted the freedom of being able to do the things that I wanted to do, when I wanted to do them. Like most children my age, it never works out that way.

2
Daddy's House

This is where my life would lead me to the man that would change my life forever. My mom had a tight whip on me, but it just wasn't enough to get me to fly right, and tame that inner demon within me, not an inner demon that was instilled in me, but one that grew from my trials and tribulations of life. I had just turned 15, a year had past and I had changed from this blossoming child to this unknown person who fought life, and the people around me including my parents. I was confused in life now, not seeming to know what path to take anymore. My path was dark and I couldn't see in front of my face, but on the other hand, I knew just what to do, so I thought.

The path I chose was the dark one; and I don't believe it was based on how I really felt about life; it was my interpretation of it. It was built from life issues, and I thought that I was being punished by God on what I was going through in my everyday struggle. I was always the life of the party, with a great sense of humor. I had a love for laughter and a strong desire to please everyone around me. I had always felt the need to prove myself to every body, and to show others I am not really what you see or think I am on the outside. I wasn't sure of what people thought of me when they looked at me, but I was warm on the inside and cold on the outside. Since, I had to fight every day; this caused me to get into a lot of trouble. Not because I wanted to, I just had a new view on life that I needed to have my guards up to protect myself.

My mom just couldn't take it anymore so she sent me to go live with my dad. That was a hard thing for me, to leave my mom. Even though I caused her a lot of pain, I loved her. My issue was not with her, my issue was with life, my fight was with life. She couldn't tell though, because I didn't talk to her, I didn't tell her my struggle. If I knew then what I know now, I would have listened to my parents, because, everything they told me came to past. In my own light, I thought everyone was against me. If I didn't hold this pain inside me for so long, and talked it out with my parents' my life would have went in another direction. I would be that attorney that I so wanted to be. I would find out later that it is very important to talk out your feelings, because when you hold them inside to long, you will and you can, self destruct.

My mom knew that my dad could whip me right into shape....at least she thought. I love my dad, but I felt in so many ways my father deserted me and my brother. Yes, he was around, but not too much. He would come around mostly when we got into trouble, and that bothered me. I had so much hurt and anger for him, because I wanted him to be there all the time. He had re-married, and his new wife had a daughter the same age, and only six days younger than me, and born in the same year. My anger with him was because he raised her, and didn't raise me.

A lot of anger in my childhood came from many aspects within my life. I love my father and today I still thrive for that love, that I so wanted when I was younger. I was hated so much at that time by my step mother that she told me that "I would never amount to anything". That hurt me, really hurt me, because I felt my father should have stepped in at times, but he never did. That pushed me away from my dad, because I didn't feel he had my back. I wasn't daddies little girl anymore, I thought we should have had a bond, an unbreakable bond, because I was born on his birthday. My step mother pushed my buttons all the time; she wanted me out her house, and away from her daughter. She didn't of course want me to instill in her, what I was going through, and the things that I was doing on a daily bases. However, little did she know I didn't have to do anything to steer her daughter in the wrong direction. My little sister had her own demons she was fighting. In this transition to my dad's house I experienced my first sign of abuse, not to me but someone very close to me. This would prove to be my lesson on life, that there is another playing field out there.

3
Too Young to Be Abused

I would never forget her; she was petite and pretty as a button. She was one of the nicest persons I had ever met in my life. I seen and talked to her everyday, she was so full of laughter, and seemed to be so happy inside, so full of life. Little, did I know she had very serious issues that only pondered her from within. She was a woman before her time; she too was only 15 and had lived a hard life, way before I met her. I felt, and she even told me, she didn't have anybody but me and my sister to confide in. So one day I, my sister, and my friend decided to skip school, I joined them and we went to her house to chill out and enjoy the day, until it was time to go home. As we were walking to her house, she confided with confidence that her boy-friend was being abusive to her.

Wait What? Abusive? We didn't know anything about abuse back then. She told us that if her boyfriend was at her house when we got there, that it would be trouble. I told her "Girl, I got your back nobody is going to mess with you with me around," or at least that is what I thought. So finally, we get to her house, got comfortable, we ate, watched TV, and talked with her mom. Yes, her mom was home and didn't have a care in the world that she was even skipping school. We were there only a little time before; there was a knock at her door.

Her mom answered the door, my friend was so nervous, she knew it was him. I have never seen her that way; she was a zombie an uncontrollable child. I could see the fear in her eyes; she was pacing the floor and hesitating for her mom to open the door. She knew, what was going to happen to her, she knew that if she opens that door, she didn't know when the pain would stop. She was being beaten so badly, on a daily bases. He was stalking her when she was home or at school, because he was jealous of other guys.

Soon after, her mom opened the door and the drama starts, he walks in and immediately starts to shout at her "Where the hell have you been?" and suddenly he charged right at her, she proceeded to run around the apartment to get away from him, all while he is trying to hit and grab for her. I couldn't believe my eyes; I stood there in amazement to what I was seeing. I had never seen anything like that before in my life. No way could this be possible, this doesn't happen to people, does it? Her mother went back into her room, I was shocked to see she didn't even try to protect her little girl, as if she was scared or maybe this was something she was use too herself, and she thought that it was ok.

She just walked off as if this normal, it was nothing normal about this; I couldn't fix my lips to say that was normal. All I could think of is my mother, how she tried to protect me from the outside world and from myself, all my life. I know she would take the breath of the man that hurt me in the way that he did. Later my mom proves just that. I had this feeling about her mom after that, it made me think, and wonder why. How dare she NOT protect her child, her only child!

He went to the kitchen to get a knife and he ran after her as if he was intentionally trying to kill her, and at that moment I couldn't take anymore and I screamed at him "NO!" with such rage, because I couldn't bear it, it was so hard to watch. I ran over to stop him from hurting her, he looked right in my eyes, I knew he didn't have a soul, his face was blank, like a tablet with no words. He looked to me like he was already dead on the inside, there was no love there, and he was missing something. He told me to "Stay out of it, or he would hurt me." I am not sure what thoughts ran through my head at that time, but I do know for sure he was not going to hurt her anymore while I was around.

I couldn't let him hurt her she was my friend, her mom wasn't doing anything to protect her, so I believed somebody had too. She had been fighting for so long, she was tired, and I knew it. Knowing what I know now, things could have gone terribly wrong and we all could have been seriously hurt or even dead. So, because of my persistence at the time, he told her it wasn't over and that he would see her later, and then no one would be around to stop him, from doing what he wanted to her.

He finally left and I didn't have words for what just happened, I didn't know what to tell her, or what I could do to help her. I knew I couldn't be around all the time, so day and night I would think about her and wonder where she was and what she was going through. The abuse continued until the next experience, I had with her. This time he was on a rampage, I think he was drunk and on drugs. I can remember him calling her and he asked that she come over to his house, so he could make up with her, from the abuse he endured on her the day before. She agreed to go, but she didn't want to go by herself. So because I was her friend, I didn't want her to go alone, me and my sister went with her, not knowing what was about to happen. I didn't have a clue that situations like this couldn't be fixed, that this kind of abuse would never have an end. I thought everything would be fine, and they would make up and everything would be back to normal for her.

It wasn't long before he showed his true colors after we arrived, he was high and crazy on drugs, he tore up things and did a lot of damage to everything around us, including my dear friend. You should have seen her face, her eyes; the tears that flowed were so heavy of burden and despair. She was scared for her life, almost as if she new she may die that day. I couldn't believe what was going on around me, the neighbors were outside watching the whole thing unfold; it seemed like he was beating on her forever, and I couldn't do anything to help her. He beat her so bad that day; she was so bruised and battered. Her face was swollen, her eyes shut, lips busted, she couldn't even look at me.

Suddenly, his dad pulled up and tried to help her by trying to pull him off of her. His father was a very large man, and he didn't even have the strength to pull this guy off of her, so he called the police. Minutes later the police arrived and they arrested him on the spot and took him to jail, and she went to the hospital. I never knew after that, that I would never see my friend again, I would never know what happened to her, because I lost touch with her after that, and I pray she is not dead and gone, at the hands of the person that I seen so many times abuse her. I miss her smiles, her friendship, her desire to live, and her perseverance. I continue to think about her, I never forgot her, and I never will. Peace my friend, I miss you. I hope and pray you are ok.

4
The Meeting That Changed My Life

I too, was young and adventurous looking for love, so on the way home from school my sister met a guy, a really nice guy and much older, I know by at least five years. After dating for only a short while, I thought he was really nice to my sister; he was very good looking, and very charming. So I decided to ask him if he had an older brother. Like most young girls, that was just an innocent question. However, that was a question I should have never asked. This question would prove to change my life forever. It would be a start to the madness and the turmoil of what I had just witnessed of my dear friend, and in the end I wish I had never opened my mouth.

I would end up meeting his brother the very next day; he was tall, handsome, had a beautiful smile, his skin was perfect, nice hair, in shape, and smelled really good. He was much older than his brother, he was twenty five. It was like love at first sight he was everything I had ever dreamt of, the bells and whistles I thought I needed, we hit it off instantly. I was so excited to have a man ten years my senior, I wanted everyone to know. Especially, the girls at school, I had even warned them if they even thought about trying to talk to him, that they would get it. I was so over whelmed with getting to know this man, and wanting to be with him. I had forgotten that I was only fifteen, everything else didn't mean anything to me, and I consumed my self into him.

Every day he would meet me at school, and we would talk for hours. He would take me to lunch, take me home, but only drop me off a couple blocks away. So my dad wouldn't see him; I didn't know how my dad would have acted if he knew I was dating a man ten years older than I was. One day, I finally got the nerve to introduce him to my father, our agreement was to introduce him much younger then he actually was. Since he was ten years older than I was, we decided to say that he was only eighteen. He looked really young so it all worked out. He was such a nice guy and really respectful, so my father allowed us to date. After work he would make sure he would come and visit me everyday, I would be outside with my friends when he pulled up. I would get so excited, knowing that I had someone in my life that I felt changed my world.

I had a curfew so I would have to go in at a certain time, and he would stay outside with my friends until they had to go in the house. I can remember standing at my window staring and hating that I wasn't out there with him. I was crazy about this guy, he was my first love. He was generous and very affectionate; he made me feel special and loved. I was head over heals for him so I would do anything to be with him.

After a year I moved back home with my mom, and he continued to see me every day. So one day on our way back to my mother's house the signs of abuse that I had once experienced with my friend would begin to show, and now would happen to me. Who knew that on this day my life would change, forever? One night we decided to go visit his brother, the one my sister was crazy about, so we can do a cookout and go swimming. We just wanted a quiet day of leisure, and some quality time. Our love for each other that night had a great deal of laughs, hugs, and I felt a genuine affection, it just felt really good. Matter of fact, one of the best times we had shared since we had been together. I had school the next day so we decided to leave and head for home.

As we made our way to my mom's house we had a great conversation about life and our relationship, and what our future looked like. I was happy; I thought my life was changing for the better. So as we were traveling down the freeway, I looked over and encountered this man trying to get my attention, so much so that he was smiling and trying to catch up with our car. After I noticed what was going on, I told my boyfriend that "Men are so disrespectful; this guy is trying to talk to me; and he see that I am in the car with you."

I noticed that he didn't respond back, but he looked rather strange in the face. Nothing else was said, at that time, but shortly after he asked me "You like that don't you?" I said "What?" He said "You fucking heard me". Then his arm rose up and he back handed me right into the window of the car. My face hit that window so freaking hard; I am surprised it didn't shatter the window or even crack any of my teeth. He hit me with so much force; my face was red and bruised. I didn't know how to react to that, as it brought back memories of what happened to my friend.

First, I was in shock not sure about what just happened to me. I was so dazed and confused, until I realized that this man just hit me, and he didn't even have a reason too. Please remember, there is never a reason for a man to hit you. I knew at the time I didn't deserve that, and how dare he put his hands on me. I was a feisty spirit and a fighter, I decided to keep quiet; until I returned home, I knew that if I got to my mother's house she would protect me. I also knew if I had retaliated in the car, it could have been way worse. I was fuming with anger, so that was a long fifteen minutes to my mom's house.

When we arrive; I immediately jumped out the car and just started screaming and cursing at the top of my lungs. My mom ran out the house asking "What's wrong, what's going on?" I told her "This mother fucker just hit me!" I was only fifteen at the time, but I was so angry and hurt that he would even do, what he did to me. Immediately, he started to deny what actually happened, and told my mother that we were just playing and that he accidently hit me. (You see this is the first sign of an abuser, denial). I should have known at that time he was not the one for me. (This is where we go wrong; we love so hard that we don't even see the truth, even if it is right there in front of us.) I should have left that situation when it happened the first time that night, because this would be the first of many acts of physical abuse, so let me add by saying.

(Physical abuse is a problem, but if you're going through physical abuse, then mentally you're being abused as well) My mom had a long conversation with me that night, and she told me like any other mother who have ever experienced abuse would say. "If a man hit's you once, he will hit you again." She also told me if "It hurts the same fighting back, as it does when you're down on that ground getting beat." Those are words I should have lived by, but I didn't, because my love for him over powered the truth. Like most young girls, I was so in love, and this man was my every thing at least that is what I thought. (Ladies we have to realize Love doesn't hurt! We should not be trapped in relationships feeling overwhelmed with no power.) Enrich your lives not with a man, but your faith in GOD. A leap of faith is the only thing that can get you crossed over, do it before it's too late.)

5

Married to a Monster

After moving back in with my mom, and experiencing the hit to my face. I continued to be with this man. This was the same man that would have the nerve to hit me like I was another man. The same man that told me he loved me and that he would never hurt me. We continued to date; and he tried to prove to my mom that he was such a good genuine and honest person, with good values, and a good heart. He took very good care of me, made sure that I didn't want for anything. He kept food in our house, washed my mom's car, and did things that would make me believe that he is the one for me, the man that I always wanted to marry. That was the furthest from the truth; turns out he was a devil in disguise.

The Devil comes in many forms, he was a very handsome man, with strong model features, physically fit, a 6th degree black belt, with a killer smile. He appeared humble and had a love and thirst for life. He was a hard working man that was dedicated, who took pride in himself not being that stereotypical black man that has no job, no money, and no self respect. I loved that about him and that's what made him who he was. Or did it?

Being fifteen and believing I knew more than women twice my age; was my biggest mistake. I lived my life as if I was the parent. I did what I wanted to do, when I wanted to do it, and no, my mom didn't allow it nor did she put up with it. I was having sex and living life like I had no worries or concerns. Nobody could live my life but me, I was my own protector. I didn't need anyone. I eventually proved to myself that was not the case.

I bought a pregnancy test, because I believed I was pregnant, and no, I didn't use any protection to avoid getting pregnant; I wanted to have a baby with this man. Now, even though I wanted to get pregnant, I had a major relief that the pregnancy test was negative; something was telling me this was not the right time. Back in those days pregnancy test didn't consist of a stick test, it was a liquid, and the color would change to pink if I was pregnant. I decided to not throw the test away until my mom left the house, so I could safely get rid of it.

That thought was long gone as soon as my mother was away from the house, and yes; I forgot to throw it away. It stayed in my closet for months and months. Eventually, the pregnancy test changed colors from the negative color to the positive color of pink; it definitely sat in my closet way to long. Later it would be a relief to me that I never threw it away. It would be my master plan to get out the house and get married to what I thought was the man of my dreams.

Months later my boyfriend asked me to marry him; he wanted to have a life with me as well as a family. He said we would grow together, build together and that we would never be apart. (Don't always believe what you hear, men are good at feeding you bullshit. He gave me the world and everything in it.)

Later, I would find out that this was only to get me right where he wanted me. Which is to be his puppet; so he could pull the strings to make me do whatever he wanted me to do. Of course, I said "YES", which was the second worst mistake that I could have ever made in my life. With excitement and the upset of having to tell or even speak marriage to my parents. I didn't know what to do, so we came up with plan for him to ask them for my hand in marriage, and to tell them why it would be a great idea for us to be married.

The meeting was arranged and my father came to the house, I was so nervous. He asked my parents if he could marry me. He told my parents that he would take care of me, make sure I finished school, and went to college, if that is what I wanted to do. That he would sacrifice his life to make sure I had one. Immediately, my parents said "NO" and told us why this was not a good idea. I think pretty quickly on my feet, so the next thing I blurted out was "I'M PREGNANT"! "What?" is what everyone said including my boyfriend who didn't have a clue about the pregnancy test in my closet. My mom tells us that "We will take a pregnancy test"; I told her I already had one that I took earlier that day and I have it in my closet. I got up and went to my closet to get it, and to their surprise the test appeared positive. In my head I am saying to myself "What I do that for?"

With total heartache and disbelief from my mom, she lowered her head in disappointment. How could you? Your only 16, you had an abortion at 15! Why? Why would you do this to yourself you are so young. At that moment I didn't care, I just wanted to be with him, nothing else mattered to me. All I could see was my dreams of being married, being out of my mom's house, not having any rules, and I could do what I wanted to do, and not have to answer to my parents. As a teenager it wasn't anything that I couldn't do, I had ALL the answers. My life was full of dreams and goals, but my decisions where taking me down the wrong path.

Unfortunately, I learned dreams are sometimes just dreams, some never ever come true. You have to realize it's a big world out there, and it is not the pretty picture you may think, or the dreams you bore when you were young. This is real life, and you have to adjust accordingly.

If only my mom had me take another pregnancy test, she would have known that it all was just a total lie, I only did what I did, to get what I wanted at the time. She didn't want this and I'm sure it took her a long time to come up with the decision for me to get married. She wanted to do what was right for the baby. She knew I had just had an abortion, and being pregnant again, she didn't want me to go that route. She was not going to go through another abortion.

She told me that "You are killing babies that just didn't ask to be here!" Honestly, I think she didn't want to fight with me anymore; because, this was just only one major thing I done in my life that I shouldn't have. I have done countless more, and this only adds on to years of hard times, and struggles of her trying to guide me in the right direction. This had been a long journey, countless jobs she had to leave, just to deal with me, and my attitude.

So we are headed down to the courthouse, and she signed the papers for us to get our marriage license. Soon after we were married, I never told my boyfriend now husband, that my pregnancy was a lie. So he didn't even know that I was not really pregnant. I lived with this lie for three months until I realized that, since I wasn't pregnant my body would not show any signs of pregnancy. I hoped by that time I would become pregnant and everything would be okay. I never became pregnant within those three months, so now I had to come up with a plan as to why I wasn't pregnant anymore. (You have to realize that living a lie encourages another lie; and that you can never overcome the untruth.)

I made an appointment with the hospital, for a yearly exam. That was only a distraction for the lie that I was hiding. I wanted to show that I had an appointment with an OB-GYN, so this way I could have a valid reason to say I was not pregnant and something happened along the way to make me lose it. I came home nervous from the hospital, not sure how in the hell, I would tell my husband that I was not pregnant. I had been working on that lie for so long, and because I was so nervous. I didn't know what to say; oh my God will I get away with this?

He walked in the door, happy to see to me. I told him to sit down; I have something to tell you. As he sat down, I was sweating with fear wondering how he would respond, to what I was about to tell him. I had no clue how this was going to come out, and what would be the consequences. So I finally just told him "I went to the doctor today for a checkup, and I told the doctor that I was having pains in my lower stomach." I paused, and he said "go on," and I continued to tell him that "The doctor gave me a sonogram and he said that "You lost the baby, and that I needed to have a DNC."

He asked me "What the hell is a DNC?" I told him "That is when the baby dies, and your body has to be cleaned of the baby." "That they have to remove the dead fetus." He was surely disappointed, but he said "Don't worry we will get pregnant again," and with such comfort he assured me, everything will be fine. I was so relieved that he didn't take it much harder than he did. Unfortunately, it will be proven later, that this was just not the case. Matter of fact, it will lead to a lot of the abuse I endured.

6

Married, Dazed, and Confused

Now that we are married, and living together in his apartment in Arlington, Texas. I feel like I am finally happy and free of everything. No burdens, no more lies, and I feel protected and independent. I was spending the day cleaning and decorating my new apartment, (at least it was new to me), and then there was a knock at the door. Little did I know who was on the other side of it! Low and behold, there is a woman standing in my doorway, his ex-girlfriend, who was conveniently a college senior that lived right across the street from us, at the University of Texas at Arlington.

Hmmm, this is quite interesting, we moved right across the street from his ex-girlfriends dorm room or at least I moved in, he was already there. (How convenient is that?) She asked "Is Mark here?" I said what?? Who are you? What do you want with him? I'm his wife, what is it I can do for you? "Nothing" she said. "Just tell him I came by" and walked off. Knowing that I am ignorant and have no sense of the word, I held it in and closed the door, but my silence would not hold out for long. I sat in that apartment for twenty or thirty minutes, before I jumped up, and proceeded to the door, but something, stopped me in my tracks.

I was nothing short of a fuse that was already lit, and ready to explode. I wanted to just pounce on her and rip her ass a new one, but for some reason at that moment, I felt the need to just wait, wait till he got home, so I can ask him what that was all about. All day I waited, and paced the floor waiting for him to get home. I was going to handle this situation no matter what the outcome was going to be. After a hard days work, he walked in the door, and I immediately confronted him! Who is this bitch that came to my house? She says she is your ex, why does she feel she can disrespect me and my house; by coming by to see you?

Why the hell haven't you told me about her? Why you didn't tell me your ex conveniently lives across the street? I had countless questions, and was an emotional fireball that was ready to let loose. I felt betrayed, lied too, and that he was still seeing her. He is standing there with his mouth wide open and all I could see is teeth; he was really surprised, or at least he acted surprised that she even did that. He told me he would take care of it, immediately. I told him he better take care of it, or I will, and if he didn't, it would be some shit!

After two weeks, I am home cleaning and preparing dinner, and I find items that belong to her in my damn house. Yes, items to show that at one point in time she either lived there or she visited quite frequently. So to no surprise to anyone that knew me, I was able to find out what dorm room she was in by knocking on each and every door. I'm sure it had to be over 50 doors in this place. I just knew this was not going to be an easy task.

So, I proceeded to knock, door by door, and eventually lucked out on door number three. She answered the door. All I could see was red, and I am pretty sure she could see that I was not there to play. My blood is boiling, and all I wanted to do was drive my nails deep into her skin. I threw everything that I had found in that apartment at her, and I went for her jugular. I hit her and we started to fight, a very intense fight indeed, and after I finished whooping her ass for disrespecting me, and coming to my house. I slowly started my journey back to our apartment. I must admit that was the last encounter with her, and no other issues pursued. I prevailed once again and now I felt that my life was back on track. Until....

Months later, I decided to go for a stroll, it was the middle of the summer. I stumbled upon a kitten; well the kitten stumbled upon me. I am not a cat lover, so the kitten proceeded to follow me home. Because I am an animal or dog lover, and the kitten was so tiny and so cute. I decided to take it home with me and keep it. My husband was an animal lover too, so I knew there wouldn't be any issues to keeping this gorgeous little kitten. He told me I could keep it but I had to care for it, feed it, whatever was required. Ok, No problem, I had it all figured out. What I didn't know is that kittens are not like puppies, they are far from it, you can't train them to go outside and use the bathroom, and I had no idea what kitty litter was at the time.

Nija' is what I named her, and oh my goodness, she used the bathroom all over that house. The smell was horrible, and I just couldn't figure out what to do. My husband came home from work, and said he just couldn't take it anymore. He grabbed Nija by the throat and threw her down the stairs, attempting to throw her against the wall. Like all cat's she landed on her feet, he ran down stairs and grabbed her again and began to beat her and beat her, as if she was another man. Her small frame couldn't take it; and he beat her till she was lifeless. That was the first of many animals that I would grow to love, and they would end up dead, in the same horrible way. At this point, is when I realized that he was not only an abuser, but an animal killer too. I couldn't believe he just killed this innocent little kitten. I cried for days, and I couldn't wrap my head around what could be next?

The perfect little wife I was, I cooked and cleaned. Did what I thought was my wifely duties; I tried to be what I thought I should be as a wife. So, one day I decided to cook his favorite meal, and by the way I was a very good cook. I learned from the best of course, my mom. His favorite meal was steak, mash potatoes, green beans, and corn bread. It was a great day to relax and watch a movie, he was due to be home by 5:30p.m., and it is 5:22p.m. I rushed to make sure everything was perfect. I can hear him pull up, and soon as he enters the door, I said "Hey honey, welcome home", "How was your day?"

Apparently not a great day at all, he threw everything to the floor. I didn't get a response to what I just asked him, so I'm like "What's wrong with you?" Why in the world did I ask him that? Knowing that I knew something was wrong and that moment he would blow up at me. As always I was right, he immediately started to yell and scream at me as if I was the culprit who ruined his day. I told him "Sorry you had a rough day, but I am not the cause of it, nor will I accept you screaming and hollering at me, for something I did not do!" I made him a plate, proceeded to walk and extend it to him, and suddenly after grabbing the plate from my hand. He just threw it across the floor and asked me "What the Hell is that?" I don't want this shit, clean it up and make me something else. I immediately went off "How dare you, disrespect me like that?" I am not cooking your ass anything else, fix it yourself!

He instantly grabbed my neck and proceeded to choke me, and told me that I would get in that damn kitchen and fix him something to eat; or he would beat my ass. So unwillingly I went into the kitchen and while I was in there, I rested my hands on the counter and told myself that he would not get away with that. How dare he keep disrespecting me like this? I stand there wondering what to do next. I was so full of anger and rage, I was thinking of how I should go in there and just blow his fucking brains out. I wanted to hurt the person that hurt me over and over and over again. For some reason I just couldn't go that route, and I am glad that I didn't. His rage started to become a daily routine, a way of life. It consumed me where I could not breathe, and I was scared to get help.

I was told if I ever told anyone about what was happening to me, he would kill me and my family. I took this threat very seriously, he had proven to me many times he was capable of carrying out his promises. We had been married two years now, and I didn't talk to my family after we got married. It was my secret and I had never told a soul, my whole demeanor had changed; I had lost a lot of weight. I wasn't really taking care of myself like I use to. I was so withdrawn, scared to stay and scared to leave. My life was changing forever, my history was being engraved in what I thought was a cruel world.

I didn't believe that there was a way out, and that I too could possibly die at the hands of my abuser. It was a constant battlefield in our house; I was waking up and going to sleep being abused. Mentally and physically abused, and I was confused. I had so many questions, what is it? What did I do wrong? Was it me making him act this way? Why did he choose to harm me, all I wanted was to make him happy? It wouldn't take me long to find out that it was never me, that made him act the way he did.

Here we go again, it never stops, and I am enjoying a day of leisure, sitting in a tub of bubble bath listening to Marvin Gaye on my head phones. I started to fall into a deep sleep, and then suddenly I was awakened by a hand around my throat, and I was pushed under water violently. While I am splashing around and choking on the water in the tub, I can see his face. Not a face of an intruder, but the face of my husband. As I am grabbing for his arm to pull myself out the water, he pushes me down harder and deeper as if he wanted me to die. My eyes are burning from the soap and the bubbles, and as I look into his eyes and he looks into mine. I can feel myself getting motionless, I was losing that fight.

I could feel myself slipping away. As I look at him I can see the anger in his eyes, and his hatred he had for me. I knew at that time I was going to die, and I could feel my body falling limp, my chest is hurting from the water entering my mouth. It was so violent; I could feel death was near. Then all of a sudden as my breath started leaving me, and my body stops fighting, only then he pulls me up from the water. I am gagging terribly, coughing, and trying to catch my breath. My eyes feel like they are popping out of my head, my throat hurts from the death trap he had around my neck. While I am fighting to live, he only walks out as if nothing had happened, he had no excuse or reasoning to why he did this to me. He never does.

After I pull myself together and I gathered my thoughts. I step out of the bathroom into the kitchen. Eyes swollen I could barely see this monster; I can't even hold my self up, as I held the side of my kitchen cabinet. I ask him "Why did you do that?", "What did I do?" These are the questions that I will continue to ask myself for the next six years of my life with him. All he could say to me is "Shut the fuck up and go fix me something to eat." I stood there in disbelief not knowing what to say or what to do.

Even though I had been in this position many times before, every time it happened to me it was like new, and I asked myself the same questions. Had I become a robot to the abuse? I was amazed at how callus he was, and how he didn't have any feelings or emotions to what he had just done to me. I was frightened and scared, knowing that I almost died at the hands of the man I loved, and who I believed loved me.

I can remember countless days that I just wanted my mommy, the lady who never hurt me despite the pain I dealt her. She was there for me, and as much as I wanted to call her name I couldn't. I wanted her safe, I wanted my family safe, and I didn't want to be the problem anymore. Days were not always as bad as this one, and some days were more mental then others. Mental abuse is just as bad as Physical abuse it's just another form of abuse, and his words would cut me like a knife. The core of my soul was a dark endless hole full of dread and fear; as to what would come next. I sat every-day not knowing what was to come, or when that devil would show his face again.

See my husband in his happiest days, wanted to not only teach me things, but act as a father to me because he was ten years my senior. He felt that I should listen, obey, and do as he says when he says's it. He always told me you will do as your told, and if not you will be punished. (Men try to rule over women by trying to scare you into being weak and fragile, so they can have control over you, but that only makes them cowards) I didn't have a need for a gun, a need to learn how to shoot a gun, or even wanted a gun in my house.

However, this old country boy from Sherman, Texas insisted that I learn how to load and shoot one. There were 5 guns in our house, all were big and small. The largest being a shot-gun and the smallest being a .25 caliber. With his over powering ways it was my job to learn how to use them. Of course there was a reason for this; it was to let me know when they were cocked and ready to blow my head off. He knew as he had his fingers on the trigger, that at any time he could kill me.

It was a pretty normal night; and my normal nights are not so normal. Those nights were full of pain and heartache, even if was not at the hands of my husband. I lay sleep in bed, after a long night of worrying where my husband was. I couldn't go to sleep at night because; I was scared to be home alone. I couldn't keep my eyes open, so I would drift off, and as usual he goes out for a drink with the guys after work, and leaves me home without a phone call to let me know what he is going to do.

At 3 A.M. he wakes me up by tapping me on the head with the barrel of his .45 caliber. He then proceeds to asks me "What's his name?" "What's that mother fucker's name?" I say "Who?" "Who are you talking about?" He says "The guy you're fucking with", I told him "I don't ever leave this damn house, and how could I ever cheat?" My mouth is shut when he hit me with the barrel of the gun; he didn't like me talking back. So that was his way of shutting me up. As he is hitting me with the gun, he threatens to kill me; and then tells me "If he ever caught me cheating on him that he would kill me." I heard that so much that, I just wanted him to just finish the job. Hell, if you're going to fucking kill me just kill me and let me die. That was a night like so many other restless nights that I told myself things couldn't get any worse, yet they did.

7

The Devil Is a Lie

You see abuse had become a major part of my life; this was almost an everyday event for six years. This day was, well I felt a pretty normal day, school was out for the summer and I was home preparing dinner. Even though I had bad days, he would love on me, laugh with me; and make me feel like a woman should. I was full of laughter and having fun with my husband, getting lots of hugs and kisses. I felt a genuine compassion from the man I desired to be with. (Weird I know)

So as the day moved on, we get a knock on the door. It is my brothers' girlfriend; so I go outside and talk with her. She was having a bad day, and wanted to talk to someone. Our conversation was great; we talked about everything under the sun. Hours and hours went by, until we were interrupted by my husband. Apparently, our conversations were way to long, because he came outside and stepped right in between us.

He forcefully told her "You need to go home" and then told me "I need to get my ass in the house." While he was telling her to go, I was behind him motioning her to get my mom. I knew what he was about to do, and I was scared to death. So she hurried off to my mom's house. Oh my god, he was so upset that I had not completed my homework, I know that wasn't really it. I was really what he wanted me to do, that he was not in control of the situation. He turns around and tells me to get into the fucking house. As soon as walks into the apartment he starts to yell at me "You know you should be in this house doing your homework, instead of running your damn mouth," then right after that the conversation changes to "What were you talking about, and were you talking about me"? He was very jealous and insecure; I couldn't understand that, as he was able to hold his own.

Instantly I knew this was not about homework, this was about his feelings. I guess he had a guilty conscious, because of his cheating ways and what he put me through. So as soon as I opened my mouth to talk, he hit me; down to the floor I went dazed. He then picks me up by my throat, and hit me repeatedly over and over again. I'm dazed, confused, and again wondering what I did to deserve this. He aggressively began to pick my thin 108 pound body up over his head, and slams me into our dining room table.

My table at the time was a sturdy wood table with glass insets. As my body falls to the table, I feel my body become one with the table, I am falling in slow motion, as my skin begins to tear as the glass rips my skin and blood begin to flow from my body. My back feels as if I was struck in the back by an 18 wheeler. Sharp pains shoot throughout my body, I just knew my back was broken, I couldn't move. My face battered and swollen feels like I have no teeth, I am numb yet I am in so much pain. My eyes are watery and I can barely see anything. My head is pounding from the pressures inside my brain.

All this while he is still beating me, my life is flashing before my eyes. I have seen this vision so many times, and it is a different one every time. Oh my GOD! I can't move, my body is limp and as I lay there I can see him but I can't hear him. Everything around me is silent, I can't hear a thing. He is still yelling at me, not sure what he is saying, because I am in a trance and still very dazed. I find myself crawling to the couch from our dining area, not knowing what to do or what is going to happen next. As I started to crawl I am getting kicked in my side, my neck, and my face. Finally, I make it to the couch; I lay there half naked as he continues to beat me out of my out of my clothes.

I pull myself up to the couch with all I had in me, and preceded to lay down to try and regain my energy. While I lay on the couch, I realized that I didn't have on anything other than my panties and my bra. Where are my clothes? I had on a pair of blue jeans and a t-shirt. While I am laying there motionless, he is still screaming at me at the top of his lungs. He continues to hit me in my face with his fist, in a downward motion into the couch like he was trying to burry my face in it. I can see him but I still can't hear anything. Blood is running from my nose and staining the couch. Tears running from my eyes and is becoming one with the blood. Suddenly, I hear loud sounds of banging and screams coming from the door. "Open this door" "Open this fucking door".

Those screams are from my mother, I am sure she could hear him screaming at me as she is walking up to the door. While she is banging and screaming, he is telling me softly to "NOT to open that fucking door." I felt diminished and I couldn't move anyway, I was in so much pain, and I felt I couldn't even make it to the door if I tried. All of a sudden he says "Open the fucking door." Only this when he realizes that she wasn't going anywhere, and if he didn't let her in she would call the police. If you knew my mom, you would know she was coming through that door one way or another. I started to make my way to the door, what felt to be a journey, after falling from the couch. I started to slowly crawl to the door, it was so intense, and I didn't know if I would be shot or if he would start beating me again.

Finally, I made it to the door and reach up to unlock and open it. I see my mom, she was my angel that I prayed for, and she was staring at me with such pain in her eyes. The conviction in her eyes as a parent to see me sitting there on the floor looking up at her helplessly, her eyes told her story. She walks in, her purse is hanging off her arm, her other arm is resting within that arm, and her hand is supporting her chin. She enters, and all she could fix her lips to say was "Mark, Why?" as she looked at him and he stares back at her, he says nothing.

When he had nothing to say, she just couldn't handle it anymore, she then reaches deep into her purse, as to pull out something, my eyes still blurry. I can't really see, until she pulls out her gun. She pointed it directly at him, and at that moment I could see the pain, the anger, the hate she had for this man, because of what he had done to her daughter. I know my mom, and at that moment she loved me despite my pain to her. She was my protector she came to fight for me.

I wasn't ready for what was next; he picked up his twelve gauge and pointed it directly at her. He only had it near him, because he had already threatened my life before she got there. My eyes had seen death coming before, but it was not going to happen that day, and if it did it would be me not my mother. My body ached, and my soul was dead so I jumped up in between the guns and I pushed my mother out the door and we rushed out to the car.

Most people would ask "Did you go back?" and I answered "Yes I did." Why did you go back? I just knew in my heart I could change him, or I just thought that he would feel bad and it would never happen again. (This is a lie, I have lived all this time, with an abuser, and an abuser never changes his stripes.) I even thought that he loved me enough to know that he was killing me inside and out, and that he would change. Most importantly he said he would kill me and my family. None of this made since to me, until later.

He grew up in a family that I thought was loving, church going, and everything was about family. Until, I heard that his father was abusive to his mother, the word is was. As they got older in age his father no longer was abusive to his mom, so if his dad had changed why couldn't he? His family use to tell me of ghost and demon stories, that their houses were haunted, and because of these stories. I use to tell him "You are the devil; that demon must have gotten into you." You see the beatings were so horrific; they were inflicted with so much hate, no care in the world as to what he was doing to me. His eyes were blood shot red, and his teeth were like fangs, longer than most people I've seen. To me this was a sign of the devil and I knew one day the devil would show up, and so he did.

On a winter night we were home sleep, and I was awaken by something not sure why or what. I didn't normally wake up through out the night, so it was rather strange. It was really quiet and the moon was shining through the window. Everything seemed slow, and not in real time. I just remember opening my eyes and seeing him lay-ing there next to me looking me directly in my eyes. That look that he gave me, all I can say is that, it was evil, nothing I had ever seen before in my life. His eyes were open wide and his mouth revealed all of his teeth like a demon would. His eyes didn't flinch, neither did his mouth. Even though this was very strange, I thought to myself, is he playing a joke on me to scare me? I asked myself then why is he not moving, not flinching and waking up to tell me this is just a joke? Then more thoughts started to run through my mind, is the devil re-vealing himself? I jumped up and was sitting on the side of the bed, not knowing what to do next. I started to run down stairs and out the door, but I quickly realized that what ever it was, it would not let me make it out that house. My mind is wondering, traveling a million miles a min, I am so scared for my life. How do I face evil? I grew up in church, I believe in the bible and also in the afterlife. This was real and I was being tested.

Soon as that thought crossed my mind, I feel the bed move. His body begins to move feet first like a serpent. His feet moved to the end of the bed, as if someone was pulling him, and slowly his body followed. Like a snake, a serpent. I knew this was impossible for any human to do. I sat there in amazement, and shaking like a leaf, and not knowing what I could do to get out. Meanwhile, his face is still eyes wide and all his teeth are showing. He had such a demonic look, I can't explain it, but I do know whatever it was - it was evil. His body slithered like a snake backward to the floor, leaving his head rested against the bed. He was in a fetal position, with his head facing the same way his body came to rest.

Out of fear of the unknown I'm not sure what made me do this, but I got up and walked around the bed and sat next to him. The fear I had within me was not like any other fear I had ever experienced or felt in my life. "Lord I praise your holy name, what do I do to remove myself from this?" I grew up in church and have faith in GOD, and I knew that he had my back, in whatever position I was in. When I became of age I didn't go to church anymore, but I continued to pray mostly when I needed him, and more so than I ever thanked him for the many blessings he had given to me.

My faith in GOD, however, showed me that I needed to pray, and I all could remember is that I started to rub his head very slowly. I began to pray over him not knowing what I was saying, but it came natural and it was easy for me to do. I began speaking in tongue, as I didn't know the words that were coming out of my mouth. These were words I had never heard of or spoke before in my life. As I rubbed his head and prayed over him with such conviction to remove that demon, I rocked and rocked out of fear. I can't even tell you at that time how I felt, I was in another place.

However, I did know GOD was with me and he didn't forsake me when I needed him. I started to have a warm feeling of being safe and not fearful anymore. As soon as I started to feel that way the devil stepped in. He wakes up out of this trance, and immediately jumps up and tells me "Bitch you trying to kill me?" he says "Why am I here on the floor?", "Why do you have your hands on me?"

He had no clue as to what just happened to him, no memory at all of it. I tried to tell him what happened, but he wouldn't listen to me. He continued to scream and holler at me, as if I was trying to really kill him. He told me that he would kill me before I ever got a chance to kill him. He never knew what happened to him, when I told him it did, he didn't believe me.

8
My Love for Animals

All my life, I have had a love for animals, wanting to be married, having children, and just being happy and content. I believed at the time, I wasn't really being loved by my husband; there were no more hugs, kisses, or intimacy that meant anything, so I gravitated to something I could love and it could love me back, so I got a puppy. Something that I could hold and love, that wouldn't control or hurt me. This was a way of getting rid of the grief from the abuse I was receiving; this was something to make me feel better especially, when I was in a depressed state especially after my beatings. Through all of this turmoil in my life, I grew to put everything in the back of my head instead of dealing with it. So mentally, I was able to put it in the back of my head and store it away. I was too scared to leave so over the years this had become a way of life for me.

I went outside for a walk to the mailbox, and I met a lady that was getting rid of poodle puppies. She had just one left, and it was the runt of the litter. She asked me "Would you like one, she is the last one?", "It would really help me, because I can't keep her", I asked "How much do you want for her?" she said "Nothing, I am giving them all away for free." this was the best thing I had heard in a long time. So I said "Yes, I would love to take her off your hands." This puppy had very curly hair, shiny black hair, and beautiful black eyes. I fell in love with her as soon as I picked her up. That puppy became my best friend, and I spoiled her to death literally, she was with me every minute of the day. So one day I decided to do my nails, and I had the polish remover out, and was sitting in the bathroom taking off my nail polish. She was sitting right under the toilet which was her favorite place when I was in the bathroom.

I hear the front door open and my husband called my name. I say "I'm upstairs in the bathroom", he comes up and immediately starts yelling at me. I don't even have a clue as to what it was about. He just grabbed me and started hitting on me, and with all the commotion going on the polish remover spills and falls right on top of my puppy, right in her eyes. She starts to whelping, but it definitely didn't stop him from hitting me. So I try to stop him and run to her aid, and he says "Fuck that dog!"

I was so mad and hurt that he didn't care that this puppy was in so much pain. I knew I had to get to her to flush her eyes with water, so I fought my self away from him and ran back into the bathroom. I picked her up and immediately put her under the running water to wash her eyes out. Then I started to think about how much pain I was in. So I told her, we would get through this together, as if she was just like me, battered and abused.

Months past and you couldn't break us apart; she followed me everywhere I went. She slept when I slept, she ate when I ate. I walked her throughout the day, and she never got enough hugs. This was too much for him though; he felt that this dog was taking too much of my time, and that he wasn't getting anything from me anymore. So he started to be really mean to the dog, so every time the puppy made a mistake in the house or barked while playing, or hell he didn't have to be doing anything. My husband would just kick it or hit it, I felt myself having to protect it all the time. I even asked him "Are you jealous of this dog?" apparently that wasn't the right question to ask.

So I received a slap in my face, and was told "Don't you ever say any shit like that to me again!"

That only made the abuse for the puppy even worse. There was a constant hit and kick, so much so that the puppy wasn't playful anymore, she was so fearful of him that she would run to me for comfort and for me to protect her. Until, one day the hit was too much for her, and she died. All I could do is pick her up and hold her lifeless body, this was my baby, this was who I grew to love and she was taken away from me.

That is all I knew at the time, this killing was like anything else that was going on with me and him, there was many more deaths to come. You see the beatings that I was receiving, made me lonely and sad. I would get a pet, so I could love on and it would love me back. Even though I couldn't talk to it, it was my way of dealing with what was happening to me. That was the only thing I had close to me to help me deal with everything I was going through. When I lost one pet I would get another one. This man was angry, at what, I don't really know. I have learned that throughout the years. This man had an inner demon that needed to be dealt with. To be honest, I am not sure if it even registered to me at the time, that when I get a new pet, that they would soon be dead. I know he did what he did to them because I had grown to become so attached to them and not him.

As time goes by I would began to feel lonely again and not sure what to do with myself, so to the classified adds I went; seeking a companion something to love and keep near to mem so I don't have to deal with the pain not only on the outside but inside as well. I found a beautiful red Chow, he was so cute and furry, a little fur ball. He was playful and loving, and he became very protective over me. His instincts were on point, he knew when things were about to happen. He would start to growl at him whenever he approached me. My husband didn't like that, it seems to me that he took it as; she is my woman not yours. In my mind I am thinking it's just a dog, but in his mind he sees it in a different view, and because of this. He treated this dog with so much hate more so than the other dogs that I had. When we left the house for the day, I would tie his leash to the stairs. So he wouldn't go around the house and tear things up. My little Chow was not so little anymore so he would chew through the leash, and tear up things like shoes, or whatever he could find to fit in his mouth.

One day we came home and the house was a wreck, the dog had chewed up shoes, the side of the bed, and the stairs. My husband was livid, he was cussing and fussing, and his anger turned toward the dog. He tied him up again, and began to beat him with his fist over and over again so much so the dog is barking and in attack mode, and trying to bite him as he continued hitting him. I am sure that made him even more upset as the blows got harder and harder. He grabbed the dog by the neck and started to choke him. I just felt so bad for him, he seemed to be abused more than I was.

So one morning I let him out, like I always do and he ran away. I searched and searched for this dog all morning, so my husband decided to help me look for him. I wasn't sure why so he jumped in his car and started looking for him. Not sure why he felt the need to do this, because he had tried to kill him every chance he got. I couldn't find him and neither could he, he came back home and said "no luck." "I couldn't find him."

So on my way to work that day. I could hear a car skid on the freeway, and I heard a dog scream in pain. I instantly thought the freeway! I was right under the bridge, so I get on the freeway and make a u-turn, and there he was in the middle of the freeway. I can remember him laying there; his fur is waving in the wind. I knew I had to get him before someone else hit him. I got out and ran to him and pulled him to the side of the road. My husband had no respect for life or anything in it.

9

School's Out for the Summer

While in school I never looked forward to the summer, because most kids my age would be excited to be out of school. They can travel or just enjoy their time off; it wasn't like that for me. My summers consisted of sitting at my husband's job all day from eight to five in his car, everyday in the hot summer months. You see my husband says he wasn't jealous, but his actions proved that wasn't the case. He didn't want me at home all day by my self, and he say's that he wanted me to be close to him. I knew that was a lie, he just wanted to control me.

He didn't want me to meet anyone else, so I wouldn't leave him. I told him "I don't want to sit at your job all day in the car!" and he got very upset and told me that I didn't have a fucking choice, so get a fucking book or a magazine, and enjoy it!" This man was so controlling he didn't want me to see my family or have any friends. I couldn't have a social life; it was either home or I had to be with him. He worked at a carpet warehouse, a very big place with big tractor trailer trucks coming in and out the trucking bay.

I would sit there day in and day out, daydreaming about life, and what it could be if I was free from him. All I had then were dreams and hopes that my life would be different. I would think about what most girls think about, being whisked away by a prince and living happily ever after. Yes, I use to dream a lot about happiness, because I didn't know what that was anymore. In my heart I was miserable, not happy with myself, and all I wanted was just to be loved. I prayed all the time for GOD to show me a way out. Lord please make a way out of no way, give me an end to this madness. As I sit in that car I could see the sun rise, it was so beautiful, and it would calm me. The breeze that came through the window was so perfect. These were my happy thoughts; this was the time of the day that I loved being where I was. At those moments in life, that was the time I had with my Lord, a moment of solitude, a time to ask him for forgiveness, change, and thank him for what he has done for me already.

I had to prepare myself for days like this; this was eight hours a day, five times a week all summer long. Flashbacks of my life were my movie screen, some moments of happiness but mostly resentment. What did I resent? I resented the decisions I made, who I married, my way of life; and the road I was on. The road was sending me on a path of destruction a path of suicide or even murder. I was controlled by him on so many levels and scared to find a way out, but it didn't stop me from dreaming. I could see the forklifts loading the trucks, but in the back of my mind it was darkness, confusion, and sadness. I was in a world I didn't want to be in, but I was held back by what I thought at the time was love.

I was confused; I couldn't answer my own questions, or ask any-one else. He would come to the doors of the warehouse to watch me or see what I was doing. He would smile at me and waive, even blow me a kiss. In my head I am thinking I don't want you, I hate you for what you do to me. I had these thoughts in my head; I was feeling trapped and not knowing how my day would end. Not knowing when that next hit would come, or when I would be chocked, get a black eye, or a busted lip.

This is how I lived, I was in constant fear everyday, but I always smiled on the outside. No one knew what I was going through I was scared to talk and tell anyone anything. I was imprisoned without the four walls, but it felt the same. Since I had learned to put my bad experiences in the back of my mind, Smiling made me strong, it gave me a since of release. I even smiled when I was being abused, mental or physically. He would call me crazy, and he was right, that is what I had become.

By the middle of the day, it became increasingly hot. I was not allowed to run the a/c in the car, as it would run up the gas. Still with all the windows down, I was burning up. So much so, my clothes were wet with sweat, my hair was stuck to my face, and my clothes stuck to my skin. I felt the need to pass out everyday; it was just too over whelming. I would have to get out of the car to stretch my legs; which would hurt because I was sitting for too long. I definitely shouldn't have done that, as I was standing and stretching outside the car. He came up behind me, and grabbed the back of my neck, and shoved me into the car. He held me down to the arm rest in the car and asked me "Why the hell are you outside the car exposing yourself?" "You are a whore and you want men to look at you." All this while he was pressing so hard I couldn't breathe.

I tried to push away and he pushes me down even harder with every thrust. I tried to scream and tell him I wasn't trying to do that, I was just stretching. I just couldn't get it out, but I could feel myself getting weak and I started to slowly stop fighting. All I could see is my life flashing before my eyes. I couldn't see him, I couldn't look him in his eyes; so if he had killed me. I wanted him to see that look I had, so it would live with him and haunt him forever. All of a sudden, he just let me go, my legs were hanging out the car door, and he shut the door really hard on my leg. He then walks away and I could hear him say "Get out again and I am going to kill your ass", all of this happened because I was cramped up in a hot car that I didn't want to be in, in the first place.

You see I couldn't even get out of the car to excuse myself, unless

I asked permission. There were no port o potties out side for me to use, so I would have a roll of toilet paper in the car, and go behind the car when I needed to go. Yes, this happened in the middle of the day in front of his job, and his co workers. I am not sure if anyone seen anything, but I am pretty sure someone did, and they did nothing to help. He got in the car that day after work as if nothing happened. He leaned over and gave me a kiss, and asked what we were going to have for dinner. (You see this was not new to me, this was all the time, an everyday event.) I chose this life; I chose this man as my husband, because I was so young and dumb and thought I knew it all. I wished I had listened to my mom, because if I had, I wouldn't be going through this.

Besides me sitting in the car everyday, I was also told that I had to sit outside with him while he worked on the car at home. He was a smart man when it came to cars; he could take out a motor re-build it and put it back in flawlessly. He was in too cars a lot; especially low-riders, cars that move up and down and sideways, with the push of a button in the console of the car. This was his prize possession he loved this car more than he loved me, and he did everything to protect it even if it hurt me. He loved this car so much that he slept very light; he could hear a pin drop in his sleep. One night he woke up in a panic, and he awakened me by hitting my arm, and with a slight whisper he said "Get up; someone is trying to steal my car!" So still half sleep I slowly got out of bed, and by this time he is already at the window looking at the people trying to steal his car; and at his side is his twelve gauge shot gun, cocked, loaded, and ready to shoot. Then he slowly raises the window, he did this so he could position the gun where he wants it, he asks me to hold the window up because the hinges on the window didn't work anymore "hold it steady" he said, don't move." He picks up the gun and points it out the window.

I look out the window and see about seven guys surrounding his car, trying to figure out how they are going to steal it. The window we were in had a huge window seat, so I had to bend over just to hold the window up. Because, of the position I was in, I was holding the window with my finger tips while standing on my tippy toes. All while he is still trying to point and aim, I am not sure to which one he was aiming for, but this man was good at shooting targets and not missing anything. My fingers started to sweat and suddenly my finger slips, and the window falls down really fast. It falls and hits the gun, knocks it down into the window seal, this is happening while he is trying to fire the gun. The gun jams! The thieves down below hear this commotion and apparently sees the gun, and start shooting into the apartment. All I could remember is falling back onto the bed, and hearing him call out "Are you hit? You've been hit!" I am like "What?" everything was happening so fast.

That is when I realized that I had been shot. The bullet came right through the wall of our studio apartment; the top part of the apartment was not made of brick. So it was very easy for the bullet to penetrate through the wall. It hit me in my left knee and pushed me back onto the bed. I didn't feel it when it happened, and I didn't even know that I was shot until he told me. Reality didn't kick in until he said "Your leg is squirting blood" As I lay there in agony, I try to hold my leg to stop the pain, until it became numb and I couldn't feel anything. The top part of my leg is numb, but my knee is hurting like hell. I felt like I had a big whole in my knee, the gunshot shattered my knee and broke my leg.

While I am lying there, I just feel like everything was moving in slow motion. I could see my husband running around trying to call 911, and looking for a towel to put on my leg to stop the intense bleeding, blood squirting from my leg with every heart beat. I could feel my eyes roll into the back of my head, and I was trying to keep my eyes open. Not sure how I was feeling at the time, because I had become totally numb. Then all I could see was a bright light, and it was shining right on me, and I started to blink. I knew that they were there to help me, and as soon as I realized who they were I started to pass out, it was the paramedics.

As they came closer to me I could see them, but only a silhouette. I'm motionless, and everything seems to be a blur. I hear them ask me my name, not sure what I told them. Then he asked what year it was, and I think I told him 1987. This incident happened in 1990. He asked me who the President was, and I told him I didn't know. I can remember him saying "She is going into shock". So I was immediately rushed to the hospital. I had to have over 50 staples in my knee, the bullet remained in my leg, torn tendons, and I couldn't walk for six weeks. Well at least that was what the doctors told me, but that quickly changed. A week after I got out of the hospital, he took my crutches from me, and told me I didn't need them. I would have to climb the stairs and walk on my own so it would heal faster. Amazingly, he had me walking in two weeks.

I told this story, because this is a man that didn't care about my life, love or respect me enough to not put me in any kind of danger. I could have easily been killed, but then when I thought about it. I had been dead so many times before, but I knew GOD hadn't given up on me just yet.

10

Battered and Nowhere to Go

My senior year of high school, we moved from the place where I was shot. We had found a nice three bedroom home, close to my school. I was pretty excited about it, it gave me change something different and I thought I was able to leave a lot of bad memories behind. Until, one night we went to have dinner with his family, so I got pretty dressed up. Had a great time no issues or arguments, so of course I thought this day was a good day, and to my surprise that was not the case. Again, we are in the car on the way home, and he asks me a question. It was a disrespectful question, so I got upset and snapped at him. That was never a good thing, I couldn't talk back or show him any signs that I was upset, because then I would be disrespecting him. A man like that you can't say what's on your mind, or snap back at them, because an abusive man enjoys control, and if he feels he is not in control, he will gain control one way or the other.

He back handed me, he hit me so hard that my head felt like it snapped from my neck. It happened so fast, as they always do. No matter how prepared you are, and because you know it's going to happen it still takes you by surprise. As my head comes down from the impact, I lay my head in my hands to bring comfort to the unspeakable pain I was in. This is while he is still arguing at me, as always, I was in a space, where everything was blurry and dark. My eyes are closed; I could feel my heart pumping and the pounds of pressure beating in my head, it felt as if I was going to pass out. I could feel the blood leaving my body, as it ran from my nose. It was running like a faucet, heavy and fast. I was choking and gasping to breathe and no matter how hard I tried to clench my hands together to hold the blood I could feel it pouring through my fingers into my lap. I had on a wool skirt so it held the majority of the blood, but I wouldn't know how much until I got out of the car.

The car stops in the drive way, and I couldn't move. I was stuck in that same position I was in, when he hit me. I was trying so hard to not bleed over everything because I knew that too would set him off. He get's out the car and comes around to the passenger door and tells me to get out, so I start to turn my body and stick one leg out the car. I could feel the blood running down my legs. Now as I position my other leg, to get out, I stand up and a very large amount of blood falls from my lap to the ground. Plop! It was so heavy that it splashed on his clothes. My nose is still bleeding profusely, so he tells me "Hold you're fucking head up, and go into the house and clean your self up", "Then come back and clean this shit up".

I walked into the bathroom and immediately rinse my face with cold water to stop the bleeding. When I rose up to look at my self in the mirror, I see a face that I have seen so many times before. I just keep asking myself "Why?" I jumped into the shower to clean myself up and all I could do is just stand there, and let the water hit my bruised and batter body. Again I was in a trance that I had become accustomed to. The water is running from my face down my body, and as I look at the bottom all I see is RED, the floor of the shower is full of blood. It felt to me at the time, that I was washing the pain away. I am still pretty scared when I got out of the shower, not knowing what he was going to do next? Is it over, is this my last day to breathe and see my family, maybe even a hospital stay? God has been on my side all this time, and I felt the need to survive through him. Out of all these years God continues to bless me with life. You see he gives you trials in life, to see what you are going to do with it. I was definitely being tested, because I hadn't quite figured out what my purpose was just yet.

Once I had cleaned up I walk outside with a bucket full of water and a broom. So I can clean up the mess I made. All I could say is "oh my GOD" I walked out the front door onto the porch. It was so much blood; I couldn't believe that I wasn't dead! It was a huge blood clot about a foot in size. I just couldn't believe that I had lost that much blood, and I was still walking this earth. As I am cleaning the drive way he comes out of the house to check on me to make sure I was doing what I was suppose to do. He then orders me around with no hesitation, all while some neighbors are in their yards doing yard work looking at me, shaking their heads. He had no respect for me, or himself, he would then ask them "What the fuck you looking at?"

This was just another day of abuse; this was normal an everyday event. So he continues to stay out everyday after work with his cousin, until all hours of the night. My days and nights are different, some are good and some are bad. For some reason every night that he was out, I always worried about him, if he was hurt, if he was cheating, if he was in jail. It never mattered he didn't care what I thought; all he was worried about was drinking and having affairs. He told me he was angry with me, because he wanted a baby with me and I couldn't have one. A couple years into our marriage I told him the truth about the fake pregnancy; and for some reason I just would not get pregnant. He told me that he probably would not have made the decision to get married if he knew I wasn't pregnant. He said he thought I did it to trap him. Which I did! You see in our minds we think we can trap a man and think or believe that because a man is with you everything will be ok, that is not the case. Did I bring this situation on myself? Is how I'm being treated my fault? I began to believe that I brought this on myself, and I had to figure a way to fix it. My way of trying to fix it, was to get pregnant again. That was now my focus, so for three years that's all I tried to do is get pregnant, but for some reason it never happened.

Like any other night he stayed out again, I was on the couch with every light on in the house. Watching TV and covered up, I laid there wondering what he was doing, and what was going to happen when he gets home. I finally fall into a deep sleep and was awaken by being beat in my face with fists, his fists. He grabbed my neck and pulled me up off the couch, and proceeded to beat me all around my house. While he is beating me, he is saying "Why aren't you getting pregnant?" "You are on birth control, aren't you?" "Who are you sleeping with?" Look, after what I had done before I felt like God was teaching me a lesson, because this was 3 years later, and I never ended up pregnant, I wasn't on any form of birth control.

In his eyes he didn't see it that way; he thought I was still lying to him; at least that is what he told me. The beatings that I was receiving were not because of a lie, he was the one with the issues. The issues he had were bigger than me not having a baby. He had every chance to let me go, and never see me again, leave me where he found me. Ladies we have to take a look at the bigger picture, men who beat women are just people with really major issues, and the majority of the time he can't be fixed. Sometimes we don't figure this out until it's' too late.

So he continued beating and screaming at me from the top of his lungs, telling me how he was going to kill me, and putting his gun in my face. I was beaten so badly that night I could barely walk or even see in front of me. When he was done, I went into the kitchen to clean, and while I was in there, I was in constant thought of how I would kill him, and that night gave me a since of courage to live, and for him to die. When I dried the dishes, I placed a cast iron skillet my mom gave me under the cabinet on top of all the other pots and pans, so I could get to it. I was planning to beat him in his sleep with it; and I wanted him to never wake up. My mind was made up, and it was time to stop the beatings. I just couldn't take it anymore, my body was so fragile.

I turned off the lights in the house; it was pitch dark other than the moon that was shining through our bedroom window. Normally, he was a light sleeper, and woke up through out the night to check on his car, especially if he heard any weird noises. This night however was different he never woke up, so I crawled out of bed creeping slowly into the kitchen to get my weapon of choice. I sat it on top so it would be easy for me to get to it, it made a rumbling noise, and I remember that my body just froze. Oh my God he is going to hear me and wake up, and beat me again, but he never woke up. I slowing proceeded to walk back to my bedroom, walked around to his side of the bed, and slowly lifted the skillet right above my head. You see this was very difficult for me because I was only about 100 pounds. As I struggled to hold the skillet, I came down with as much force as I could with my little frame. Bam, he woke up in a daze not knowing what happened, but once he found out what I did or what he thought I was trying to do, he beat me again. This time it was much worse.

It was nothing for him to come home everyday and beat me, it was almost like he really enjoyed doing it, seeing me in pain. Nights I would wake up to his hands around my neck, or being hit in the face, or smashing my face into what ever I was laying on. Twisting of my arm into my back, slamming me into walls, pulling my fingers back till I screamed in pain, and he did this with such a fierce and devilish look in his eyes. To me he was the devil, evil and had compassion to do wrong to me.

11
Moving North Has a Downside

We decided to move again, to the north side of town and close to a nearby lake. This time we chose an apartment on the third floor. Very nice and roomy, one bedroom; I liked it, it was really cozy. I had really started to mature in age, so for my 19th birthday I decided I wanted to get drunk. I don't necessarily believe the drinking was only due to my birthday, because I had issues big issues, and I believed I wanted to wash them away by drinking. I wasn't sure how I would feel drinking; I just observed that every body around me had issues, and they didn't have them when they got drunk.

I wanted to drink away my problems too; maybe life would be so much easier for me. I could drink my self to sleep and never wake up again. Before I decided to drink, I taught myself how to put my problems in the back of my head, as if nothing ever happened. Those were memories that I didn't want to remember, I felt by burying my pain, it wouldn't hurt, so I tried to mentally wash away my pain, the bruises, the cuts and scrapes, and a hard realization that I was just married to a monster.

To get away from my thoughts of being in the house alone, I would go outside and sit. Enjoy the breeze and watch people go by, I would wonder where they were going or where they were coming from. I would sit back and dream of a new life, and would I ever get to leave this dreary place. I wanted to be whisked away, by a prince so he could take away all my troubles. It is easy to dream such beautiful dreams, but it's even harder for them to come true. I started to make friends and they would sit outside with me and him occasionally. Once, he realized that everyone like me and thought I was a cool person to be around, he started to show himself more. Only because of the men that were out there as well. We had a little family of friends now, and we grilled and partied all the time. It was nothing one wouldn't do for the other.

There was a lady downstairs on the second floor that I was really cool with. She was older than me and she was in her 20's. There was an older man downstairs on the first floor; he was a grandfather figure to all of us. The nicest guy with a really big heart, if you needed anything he had your back. A friend of mine that I grew up with (Lisa) lived there as well with her boyfriend; I was so excited to see her. Finally, I had someone dear to me that was close, she had been my best friend growing up and I always knew she was hurting inside then, she too was abused as a child. I was just so happy to be with her again, and she was someone close to me, because he pushed everyone else away.

I was always in constant thought that my husband was cheating on me while away. So one Saturday afternoon, he comes in and goes right back out. My curiosity was killing me, was he going out to be with another woman? So later that day he comes in as if nothing happened, he came in changed clothes and went right outside with the guys. He brought me back something to eat, so while I am eating,

I observed his wallet on the end table. So I decided to see what was in it, and I am glad I did because I found a torn check, with all the ladies information on it, name, address, and phone number. I sat down and continued to eat till he came back in the door. He sat down on the sofa next to me; I was sitting in a chair with the food sitting in my lap. I asked him "Whose number is this?" and he went off! "What the fucks are you doing going through my wallet?" Immediately, he moved closer to me and hit me in my right leg, so hard that he put a dent in it; this would serve as a memory for me everyday the rest of my life. The force of the hit knocked all my food out of my lap unto the floor. I immediately jumped up to run out the door, because I knew what was coming next. I figured if I run outside he wouldn't hurt me because our friends were outside.

He caught me before I could get to the door; he grabbed me and slammed my head back into the door. Just the look in his eyes was intimidating me, he was the devil, and his eyes were so red. I stood there shaking and scared for my life, and then I see him raise his other hand. He grabbed my neck and squeezed it real hard, and what felt like 5' inches he lifted me off the ground. I know I was very high, because my feet where not touching the ground. I was kicking and fighting for my life; I knew it was that time again, time to meet my maker. I knew that one day I was going to die I just didn't know when.

I felt intense pressure in my face, I felt that it would just pop wide open; my eyes bulging, I could see a faint black cloud covering my face, then it started to thicken, this time was different then any other time, because this cloud was new. I never seen this darkness before, my body didn't have control, my mind didn't have control, and I was sure I was going to die. He held me there it felt like a lifetime, until I passed out. All I can remember is that I woke up in my bed. It was 3am in the morning, and I could remember that I was eating around 3pm the day before. He had left me there he was no where to be found, not even a concern if I was dying; or even dead.

He came home later that day and continued to hold the grudge he had against me, and made me stand for hours without sitting down to listen to him. I can remember my legs shaking from growing weak; I could feel my eyes roll into the back of my head. While I'm standing there I could hear him, but I couldn't see him. I started to pass out, I could feel my body fall to the floor in slow motion, and I never felt the impact. What I found out moments later is that I woke up to him putting something in my nose, and it was hot sauce as I was waking up he was still screaming at me. That didn't stop him from grabbing me with so much force it gave me an instant headache along with the pain I was enduring from the hot sauce. I'm thinking to myself "I'm going to die tonight", "What is wrong with this man; it has to be more to this?" He has gratification in harming me in whatever way is satisfying for him.

That night I leave in the middle of the night with only what I had on, I left everything else including my purse, all I had was change to use the pay phone to call my brother to come and get me. I left the house around 2:00am in the morning while he was sleep, and I ran and ran till I ran out of breath. It was at least 6 blocks from home, before I stopped running. I just couldn't let him catch up to me. I remember running into an apartment complex, it was odd that all the lights where out that night, and the breeze ways were closed off. You couldn't go through them to get to the other side, and with all the lights out you couldn't see your hand in front of your face. So I decided to sit in one of the breeze ways to catch my breath and in case he comes looking for me; he couldn't see me. I was so tired, and my heart was beating so fast, I was trying to regain my energy.

Not 20 minutes later, I hear a noise someone walking and I could hear steps getting closer and closer to me. I didn't know if it was him or someone else. I'm thinking to myself what if it is not him and it's a murderer or rapist. I told myself I'm screwed either way. The steps are so close to me that all sound stopped like I was in a slow motion dream, and then I see him. It was my husband! I immediately stopped breathing, tried not to shake, or make any noise that would give me away; as this is happening, I see something dark in his hand. It was his 45 caliber gun; he had it in his hand as if no worry in the world. Lord I'm so scared, save me tonight Lord, save me. I knew that I would die that night. I could see the intense look on his face, my life flashed before my eyes.

What do I do now, he is in the area and I don't know where he's at, I can't be here forever; and it will be morning soon. I stayed in place until I seen daylight, and I slowly began to creep away looking for a gas station, so I could call my brother. I don't know why I didn't just call 911, well I guess I didn't call because he threatened me all the time, that he is going to kill my family one by one; if I ever told them what was going on. So why was I calling my brother, Oh my God I will be haunted by this all my life, I will never be free. I had no choice I had to call, I had to get away. Finally I made the call, my brother answered and I told him where to meet me, which was hidden because I didn't want him to find me. My brother and my dad arrived and drove me to the apartment; I stayed in the car while they went up to the apartment to get me some clothes. Of course he denied anything and everything, I eventually left with my dad and brother, but retuned later to be with this same man. No matter how many times I left, I still went back. He would talk me right back, by telling me he loved me and that he would never do it again, but it always seemed to happen again and again and again.

One cold day in November he dropped me off at work, and all I had on was a small jacket and no socks with my shoes. I didn't think to dress warm at the time because he was picking me up. All I had to do is get in the car. Right? Wrong, I worked all day that day and as usual at 9pm, I would wait outside, in front of the mall for him to pick me up. Associates that I worked with started to leave as it got later and later, so by 10pm when my supervisor was leaving, he asked if I needed a ride, I told him that I just talked to my husband and he would be here shortly. I didn't dare ride with anyone especially another man. So by this time I was cold, alone and in the dark, scared and trembling, looking to my left, my right, and behind me. Hoping no one would jump out the darkness. I couldn't stay there anymore;

petrified I decided to walk across the parking lot to the 7-Eleven to get warm and try to contact him at home.

I thought that he may be sleep, until I didn't get an answer. I put another quarter in the phone, and called my best friend Lisa to see if his car was outside the apartment. She put me on hold, and told me that she would go take a look. She came back and said "No his car is not out there" I said "ok", maybe he is on his way here right now. If you see him let him know I am at the 7-Eleven. I stepped outside the store to see if I could see him and hoped that he wouldn't miss me.

I stood out there for as long as I could about 30 minutes, I couldn't take any more of the cold, my fingers and toes began to freeze. So I went back into the store to warm up, once I was able to get the feelings back in my hands and toes. I decided to walk home, I knew the conditions were horrible, but I couldn't stay at that store any longer. I started to walk, and before I could get past the light, I began to freeze, my toes and fingers especially. I was so determined to get home as fast as I could; no matter how fast I walked the cold would slow me down. I would try to pick up my pace again, even limping in pain. My toes had frozen at this point so bad I could barely walk.

Half way there my best friend's boyfriend passes me on the street, and circles back to see if it was me. All I could say in my head is thank you Jesus, you heard my cry. He took me home, but I told him I didn't want to go there, that I will just go to their house. All while I continued to wonder to myself where could he be?

I went upstairs to their apartment and they wrapped me up in warm blankets, gave me a thick pair of socks to put on, a cup of hot cocoa, and placed me in front of the fire place. I laid there for a long time trying to defrost, which seemed like forever. While laying there I had many thoughts, mainly on where he was. Was he hurt, in jail, or dead? Never did I think at that time he could be cheating on me, or that being the reason that he did not pick me up. That was just not him, not picking me up from work. That was something he just didn't do, so about 4:00 am in the morning he finally shows up looking for me, asking if I'm ok, and begging for my forgiveness. I broke up with him that night.

We were separated for about a month before we started to talk and try to work things out. He told me that he was sorry and it would never happen again, it sounded like a broken record. I could hear the scratches on the record, over and over again. I should have known better, but I didn't. I went back anyway, and one day on my way to work which was about three miles from our apartment, a straight shot down the main street. That same long treacherous street that, I just walked down, because he didn't pick me up from work. I drove over to our apartment and knocked on the door, pretty excited to see him at that moment, until he actually opened that damn door. When he opened the door he only opened it half way, which was a sign for me that something was wrong. I automatically new that there was a woman in my house; not because he wouldn't let me in, but because I knew he was cheating on me. I just accepted it, because I thought I loved him that much. When reality hit me, I was so determined to get into that apartment.

I started to push the door in, all while he is pushing me back out; finally he slams the door in my face, almost jamming my finger in the door. I started to bang on the door again, and all of a sudden I hear her screaming at him in the background, telling him "Did you tell her, did you fucking tell her?" "Did you tell her that I was pregnant?" I was like "What?" So I started to kick the door, banging on it so hard I broke my shoe. Then all of a sudden he opens the door, comes out side and grabs me, he then picks me up and threw me down the stairs, which seemed like forever before I landed.

I was only about 110 pounds at the time, so I am airborne until I get to the third step at the bottom. When I got up I was in so much pain, all I could do was look up at him, and limp away. The all white I had on at the time was filthy, full of dirt, and my body was badly bruised. I had to go to work that day, I didn't have any time off. I was ashamed to go in to work looking like that, but I had no choice. I remember walking in and it seemed everyone was looking at me, I had a broke shoe, and I was walking with a limp. I had to buy me another pair of shoes, just so I could go to work that day.

I would later find out the reason for him not showing up, to pick me up. He didn't show up because, the woman that was in the apartment, his girlfriend, was in the emergency room that night, apparently because of complications of her being pregnant with his child. She had, had a miscarriage, something at the time I never thought I could be. He told me I wasn't good enough to have his child. So he was going to have one with someone else. This same woman was my neighbor below, her best friend. I had built a friendship with her over the years, she knew everything about me, including what was happening to me, she could hear my screams at night, and I was so hurt, and betrayed by her.

I don't know really my feelings at the time, but I was in a dark place. A continuance of the hurt and pain in my life, this was a true disappointment of the decisions that I had made in my life. Reality of it all, when is enough, enough?

12
Death after Dishonor

After all I had been through in my six years of marriage to this man; I had decided that I couldn't bear the hurt and the pain anymore. So I decided that I would kill him, definitely before he killed me. I had a twisted sense of seeing him hurt, hurt to a point of no return. I would sit at times in a daze, with continued thoughts of how and when I would kill him. This became a pressing issue in my life; so I knew that the Devil had created my way of thinking. My thoughts were dark and inviting, and I wanted to take away the pain and the turmoil that I was experiencing. I have lived this life for so long, I had learned how to push away the pain, so I would forget what I had been through. That was just my way of dealing with it. The blows to my face, my head, and my body, I just couldn't feel it anymore. My pain lived on the inside, which crippled me as a woman, and a wife.

I can remember being beat so badly one night that I went to the kitchen as he slept, and I pulled a knife from the kitchen drawer. My feelings were of despair, and hope that I could commit the perfect crime, that I could put an end to this punishment in my life. I can remember my walk was slow, at a pace that seemed to take forever. As I get into the bedroom I stand at the door looking at him as he sleeps, manifesting my next move. My heart was beating so fast, I knew that he could hear how hard my heart was beating.

Even though my heart was beating fast, everything was in slow motion. I was dripping with sweat; however, fear was not an option. I am telling myself "I must do this, I can't turn back now." I proceeded to walk around the bed with the knife in my hand; I'm trembling in fear, this knife had a long blade, long enough to cut him all the way through his body and into the bed. I didn't want him to get up; he didn't deserve to get up. All I wanted was his eyes to open and look at me, and to realize the pain he put on me, and what he is now enduring.

I am standing next to the bed, with knife in my right hand. I raise my arms high above my head to get the momentum I needed to take his life. Something took over that night; no God took over that night, because as I came down with the knife, he woke up and looked at me, and jumped out of the bed and ran into the bathroom. I chased him, screaming for him to open the fucking door. All I could remember is standing there stabbing the door with this huge knife. I was in another state, I felt nothing, and it felt as a dream, like I really wasn't there.

It was very real and if I had penetrated his heart as I had planned. I would not be here today to write about it. After several hours he came out the bathroom, scared because he had not seen that side of me. I didn't kill him that day, but if I had I would have been just like him, miserable, cruel, and a murderer. This was not the only time I tried to take his life; each time I tried he lived. It was just not his time to die, and it was definitely not my time to be a killer.

So many times he could have been dead; this time I'm standing at the top of the stairs. It is very early in the morning, around three a.m., and there is knocking and banging at my front door. "Who is it?" I said. Whoever, this person was at my door, wouldn't answer, I ran and picked up the shot gun. It was heavy and cold. I aimed it at the door, and asked again. "Who is it?" and again there was no answer. All of a sudden the door knob started to twist and turn, then jerking of the door. I hear moans and groans, swearing that I need to open the door, and right now! Whoever, was on the other side of that door was drunk and belligerent. He said "If I didn't open the door that he was going to beat my ass." and "I'm going to kill you when I get in this house!"

Screaming out of fear "Who are you and what do you want?" "If you don't fucking answer me, I am going to shoot you through this fucking door!" He finally answered and he said "It's me Mark, open the fucking door!" I stood there still paralyzed with fear, and at that moment I told myself to shoot. This would be my chance to kill him and I could claim someone was trying to break into my home. So I knew at that time I could get away with killing him. For some reason I just couldn't pull the trigger, I wanted to, but I just couldn't do it.

I opened the door for him to come in, he walked in drunk. He could hardly stand up; he is falling and stumbling, he could barely hold on to anything. All while I am just standing there looking at him, as if he was an easy target. Wishing I had done what my thoughts were, I helped him upstairs and into the bed. He helplessly fell asleep on my leg, as I was pulling him onto the bed. That night I stood and looked at him, a moment in time, it felt. I decided to lie down beside him, still looking at him wondering what I should do. Over and over I planned of his death, and so many times I could have been dead at the hands of him. At that moment I chose once again not to take his life.

13
The End to the Beginning

This is year six and the beatings were not as severe as they were before, but there were still beatings. We moved rather frequently, next our move took us to Irving, Texas into a nice townhome within a nice area. This area had everything; I would make frequent trips to the grocery store, to find things to cook when he wanted something in particular. My frequent trips to the store however, was a problem, even though he wanted something different to eat, and would send me to the store, he would think that I was cheating on him. My trips to the store were timed and if he felt I was there at the store to long, he would accuse me of cheating.

I walked into the house one day and an argument ensued immediately, because I had taken too long to get home. He asked me where I was and what took me so long, I couldn't get my mouth open fast enough to answer his question, bam he hit me right in the face. While I tried to defend myself by putting my hands up to defend my face, he hit me in my the side of my ribs; I grabbed my side and buckled down to the floor. I was trying to protect myself from the hits and the kicks; this I believe made him made him stop. I picked up the groceries and went to the kitchen to cook as planned; and I could remember just standing there, wondering and looking at the knives in the kitchen. My mind is racing, head hurting, body aching, and blood is dripping from my nose. Once again I chose the other path, and not commit the crime; that I had dreamt in the last couple of years. Life moved on as if I had been beaten or not, it was just life for me. It was a way of life, this was the norm, and I really didn't see a way out of this relationship. Until……

I had my frequent visits to the doctor's office for my yearly exams; I caught the bus to the hospital as I had always done. I walked in and sat patiently to be seen, I am asked a million questions, and then told to go pee in a cup, that they needed to do a pregnancy test. This is pretty routine at every office visit. So, I am waiting for them to call me back for my exam, after I am called. I go back and before they told me to undress the lady sits me down, and tells me that I am pregnant.

"What?" I said "I'm pregnant"? I couldn't believe my ears, all these years I couldn't or didn't get pregnant. I had lied and thought that I couldn't ever be able to have a baby, a punishment of the lie that I had told six years prior. This changed my way of thinking, I didn't care about the beatings, because while I was pregnant he wouldn't hit me, so my life as I thought I knew it was getting better, things would now change, because of this new life that we were bringing into the world. I can remember the day that I had her, I was so happy, but sad because they took her away when she was born. I was left in the room alone, and cried because I needed her. I felt like I felt when I got a new puppy; I thrived on loving her and she loving me, I had hoped that she would take away the pain and despair I had endured for so many years. Not thinking about future possibilities that the abuse would stop at me.

We bring her home and everything in the beginning was just wonderful, nothing was wrong it was like everything was perfect. It didn't last very long and within eight months; he became agitated, because of her crying all the time. As she grew the more agitated he would become, so agitated that he had her trained to not move or make noises when she was only eight months old. I had gone to the store that day, so I could make dinner. I'm standing in the kitchen cutting up vegetables to put in with my roast. It's getting close to the super bowl so it was an intense time (the playoffs); he was so into the game that he told her to be quiet. She sat there the whole first half of the game, playing with her toys and napping, when half time came, she started to get irritated, and wanted to get down from the couch. I can see that face, I had seen so many times, and I knew what was about to happen.

He walks over to her; then picks her up by her shoulders. He is literally holding her with one hand. She is screaming at the top of her lungs, as he walks upstairs. I'm not sure what to do at the time; pressure was just building in me, my baby was in trouble and scared. He reaches the top of the stairs and walks into her room. I heard a loud bang of her crib hitting the wall, and she belted out a huge scream, I knew then what he had done. I was enraged and grabbed two knives out of the knife block, and ran upstairs. I get to the top of the stairs, and she is in her crib, face is red and full of tears, crying her heart out, and calling for me.

I jumped at him with both knives in hand, not knowing what the outcome was going to be. I just knew what I had to do and that was to protect my little girl. In the struggle he takes the knives from me and proceeds to beat me for attacking him. That night was long and dreadful and I was really troubled, I had to do something. I was thinking about my life over and over in my head, the many years I had endured the abuse, and now I was seeing it happen to her. She is only eight months, she doesn't deserve that. Hell I didn't deserve that. I was not going to allow him to do to her what he had done to me, so I decided it was time for me to go.

The next day I went to work and I told two of my friends at the office, that I was going to leave my husband that night. That I needed them to be at my house at a certain time, and they were instructed not to leave me in the room alone with this man. I feared that he would attack me or hurt our baby again. My friends showed up at my house at the time that they were asked. The door bell rung, I answered the door, and as they walked in they stood on each side of me and I told him, "I'm leaving you tonight!" He looked at me and us and told me that, that was fine, but you will not be taking our daughter with you.

At that moment I had to make a decision to stay or leave. My decision was to leave, that God would watch over my daughter. If I stayed he would definitely attack me and there was a possibility of hurting her too. I went upstairs to pack my things, and my friend came with me, the other stayed down stairs with my daughter, she sat on the edge of the bed, while I packed.

Twenty minutes passed by and my friend in the room with me had to use the bathroom, I said please don't leave me here alone. My other friend was down stairs watching him, so she was nowhere to be found if anything had happened. While she was in the bathroom, he came upstairs and shut the door. I was scared not knowing what to do. He walked around the bed to me and told me that "You can leave but you can't take our daughter with you!" That was the hardest choice of my life to leave my child behind. I knew I had to get away and this was my way out, I made the decision to leave and go back for my daughter the next day. He then starts to criticize me and tell me "I was worthless!" That "Nobody is going to want you!", and he then tells me that I was lucky that my friends were here, if they were not it would be another ending to this chapter. I was able to go and pick up my daughter from his mother's house the next day; without any issues this time.

Three months later I was long gone, I was trying to replenish what I had left of life. I had bought a car and was staying safe with my mom at her house. It was his weekend to watch our daughter, so on that Sunday he told me that I could come and get her. I told my mom that I was going to pick up my daughter. She immediately gave me that face and asked "Do you want me to go with you?" I told her that I would be fine, and I went on as if I didn't have a care in the world. I just knew that he had moved on and let go. I pulled up at his mothers' house and he was on his mother's porch holding our little girl, and saying his goodbyes to his mother.

I parked in the driveway somewhat at an incline, it was a pretty day outside the sun was out, the birds chirping, and neighbors doing yard work. I turned the car off, got out the car, all while laughing and saying hello to my little girl. I pleasantly spoke to everyone, and we proceeded to walk to my car, and his mom goes into the house. I walked over to the passenger door to put my daughter in the back seat; but before I turn all the way around. He asked me "what the hell is that on your neck?' I said, "What?" He says "You have a hickie on your neck!" I told him that was no hickie and I was not even thinking about being with a man after what I had been through.

He proceeded to put my daughter down. Soon as he sits her down he punches me, and I take off running for my life. Around the car I went I know about four times. As I am running around the car I see my daughter standing in front of my car, screaming at the top of her lungs, and calling for me. She was in a state of trance, she was petrified as to what she was seeing happen. Seeing her like that must have put me in a trance for a short time, because that is when he caught up to me in front of the car.

He grabbed my hair and balled my hair into his hand, and started to bash my head into the head of my car. Everything happened so fast, I just know I was in shock. Everything as always was in slow motion, I couldn't hear anything, but I could see everything. Every blow to my head hurt a different part of my face. All of a sudden I hear his mother cries "Stop, Stop, and Please Stop!" She was then able to push him away from me. I was dazed and very dizzy, my face was pounding and I could hardly see at first, everything was a blur. I could hear his mother talking to him, I could see the neighbors standing in their yards and on the streets, however the police where never called or came to my rescue.

I will never forget those eyes and that anger that he had. He leaned against my car with his right foot posted on my passenger side door, his arms were folded and he was looking away from me. Out of nowhere he smashes my back window out of my car with his right elbow. Once I regained my senses I took off running and grabbed my daughter up like a rag doll, and threw her into the car, turned the ignition on, and burnt off. Once he realized what was happening he took off running behind my car.

I can remember like yesterday the pain and fear I still had in me when that happened. That was a long ride home to my mother's house, my daughter was crying, I was crying and the pain, oh my God the pain in my face. We finally made it home and as soon as I walk in the front door my mother looked at me, and I could see the pain and then the anger in her face. She said "Let's go!" She grabbed her purse and got to the front door and Stopped! Her pursuit was to hurt him for hurting me. She told me something stopped her, and that we would handle this the right way. So we called the police and made a report. Later I would find out from his mother that my head banging into that car, sounded like he was slamming the hood down on my car.

That night I walked into the bathroom, put my hands on the counter, and looked at myself in the mirror. The left side of my face was purple with hints of red and blood everywhere; I looked like someone out of a scary movie. Once again I had a black eye, busted lip, and what I thought was a broken nose. That person that was on the other side of the reflection is who I had become, but not who I was. I look in the mirror today and look back on who she was. She was beaten and abused. Today she is a winner and a fighter. I am no longer a reflection; now I can only reflect on what I am not, which is that scared woman in the mirror.

14
Insight

This book was written for and in honor of all the women and children, who have fought to survive any form of abuse. I am one of the lucky ones, and there are many out there that have not lived to tell their story. They are currently fighting this struggle in order to survive. Abuse is a crime, physically, emotionally, and mentally.

This form of disease kills, and it has the affect of any killer disease, such as aids. It will take you to a dark place, it will starve you from life, it will create heartache and pain, and it will chew you up and spit you out. Abuse is a cowardly act, and it comes from one person that is insecure with himself, and who wants to empower themselves to show that they are inferior.

Empowerment or Love does not come from anger, love does not hurt, and love does not produce black eyes and busted lips. If we continue to allow abuse it will never stop, we must fight against this disease and end the pain of those that fight this way of life everyday. I am a survivor; this is only part of my story. I decided to share my story to help the countless women, and children struggling to live today. You don't have to be the victim, you are actually in control, get out while you can. Do it not only for you, but your children, and go into survival mode. Life is a gift, cherish it and love yourself first. Stand against violence, stand against the history of it, and stand against today's violence as it has grown into a much larger problem.

Prayer for All Who Are Abused

You chose, O loving God,
to enter this world
quietly, humbly, and as an outcast.
Hear our prayers
on behalf of all who are abused:

For children,
who suffer at the hands
of parents whom they trust and love;
for spouses,
beaten and destroyed
by the very one
who promised to love
and to cherish them forever;
for all people
ignored, hated and cheated,
by the very neighbor
who could be the closest one
to offer your love.

Hear the cry of the oppressed.
Let the fire of your Spirit fill their hearts
with the power of vision, and hope.
Grant to them empowerment to act,
that they may not be passive victims
of violence and hatred.
Fulfill for them the promises you have made,
that their lives may be transformed
and their oppression ended.

Turn the hearts of the oppressor unto you
that their living may be changed
by your forgiving love;
and bring their abusive actions
and oppressive ways brought to an end.

Amen.

www.ingramcontent.com/pod-product-compliance
Lightning Source LLC
Chambersburg PA
CBHW030553030726
47495CB00004B/1243